The Meadow Vale Ponies

MULBERRY

AND THE SUMMER SHOW

MULBERRY

AND THE SUMMER SHOW

Che Golden

OXFORD
UNIVERSITY PRESS

OXFORD
UNIVERSITY PRESS

Great Clarendon Street, Oxford OX2 6DP
Oxford University Press is a department of the University of Oxford.
It furthers the University's objective of excellence in research, scholarship,
and education by publishing worldwide in

Oxford New York

Auckland Cape Town Dar es Salaam Hong Kong Karachi
Kuala Lumpur Madrid Melbourne Mexico City Nairobi
New Delhi Shanghai Taipei Toronto

With offices in

Argentina Austria Brazil Chile Czech Republic France Greece
Guatemala Hungary Italy Japan Poland Portugal Singapore
South Korea Switzerland Thailand Turkey Ukraine Vietnam

Oxford is a registered trade mark of Oxford University Press
in the UK and in certain other countries

British Library Cataloguing in Publication Data

Data available

ISBN: 978-0-19-273466-2

1 3 5 7 9 10 8 6 4 2

Printed in Great Britain

Paper used in the production of this book is a natural,
recyclable product made from wood grown in sustainable forests.
The manufacturing process conforms to the environmental
regulations of the country of origin.

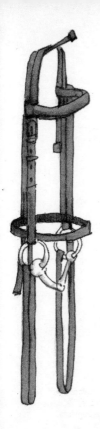

For Brie

who made us laugh

every day

Chapter 1

Sam held onto the cold steel of the gate of the barn and tried to ignore the butterflies in her stomach. All around her the stables were noise and bustle. People ran up and down with ponies and horses on their way to lessons, instructors bellowing orders as loose reins were gathered up and wayward stirrups run up out of harm's way. In half an hour, Sam was going to have to get a pony from the barn and make her way down to her first proper lesson and ride in front of lots of people. She went hot and prickly all over at the thought of

1

it and swallowed hard.

'Your sister has been our star rider in the Pony Club for some time now,' said Miss Mildew, the head riding instructor and owner of the stables, the day her mother signed her up for her first set of lessons at Meadow Vale Riding School. 'I expect to see great things from you as well.'

Sam had cringed as Miss Mildew had looked down her thin nose at her. She thought of her big sister Amy and her room full of rosettes and trophies, her neat blond pony tail floating like a banner as she soared over jumps. She wasn't Amy.

The truth was that while Sam was as horse mad as the rest of her family, they also scared her. A lot. She loved to

2

ride her mother's horse—big, chubby Velvet. Velvet never went faster than Sam wanted and always stopped when she asked. Velvet was safe and gentle and kind. Her mother told her that other horses and ponies were kind and gentle as well, and that she would feel a lot braver once she started riding lessons and learned to ride on all the different ponies at Meadow Vale.

But just the thought of riding other ponies made her want to run to Velvet's stable and hold onto one of her legs so tight that Miss Mildew wouldn't be able to prise her off. She could never be like Amy, who seemed to spring lightly onto the back of every animal and ride them beautifully, no matter how naughty or cheeky the pony was. Every time she thought of getting on a strange animal, she thought of all the things that could go wrong. They could bolt, rear, buck her off, and she would be left on the ground with a broken bone. She would never be able to stay in the saddle.

Tears pricked at her eyes, which were hot and dry from lack of sleep. She scrubbed at her face with the back of

her hand and sneaked a quick look over her shoulder. A huge chestnut-coloured horse was walking through the yard, his rider sitting casually in the saddle, just one hand on the reins. The animal was bad-tempered, putting his ears back and snapping his teeth as other animals passed him by. A trio of girls rode past on their way out on a hack, their horses

prancing and mouthing at their bits, their steel-shod hoofs slipping on the concrete. Janey, one of the riding instructors, was settling herself in the saddle of her black and white mare, Lucy, as the horse leapt and spun with excitement.

'Lucy's a bit fresh. She hasn't had a gallop in a few days,' laughed Janey when she spotted Sam's worried face. 'Off we go!' She winked as Lucy jittered and hopped out of the yard. Janey stuck to her back like glue.

Sam swallowed and turned back to the cool shadows of the barn, trying to block out the sounds of the riding school. Directly in front of her was the little herd of Shetlands that the tiniest children rode. To the right were the huge cobs that adults learned to ride on, and to the left were an assortment of ponies of different colours and sizes that the older children used. The kings and queens of the yard, the horses only the experienced riders were allowed to sit on, and the horses owned by liveries like her mother's, were kept in the grid of stables behind her. An army of children helped out at the weekend and holidays in return for free rides. They mucked out, carried water, and brushed the coats of these animals until they gleamed. At the entrance to the yard was the huge outdoor arena where lessons were held in good weather; to the back, the indoor arena with its soft sand surface. Between the two was a hive of stables, tack rooms, store rooms, and feed rooms that served the needs of 80 animals. The whole place swarmed with people. Meadow Vale was a small country in its own right and half of its population, including Amy, would be making its way down to the outdoor arena in twenty minutes to see the new kids ride in their first class of the term. If she made a fool of herself, then Sam knew she would never fit in here.

She sighed and looked at the little herd of Shetlands, who contentedly munched on their hay. Perhaps if she burrowed in amongst them no one would notice she was missing?

Just then, she was shoved hard from behind and her chest hit the top bar of the gate, the dull *clang* scattering the Shetlands.

'Oh, I'm terribly sorry, I didn't see you there,' a silky voice purred in her ear.

'But you are rather insignificant so it's hardly my fault is it?'

Sam looked up into the beautiful brown eyes of the biggest bully on the yard, Cecilia Jones. Cecilia and Amy hated each other with a passion and neither could bear to lose against the other in a competition. Cecilia was as dark as Amy was fair, with long, chocolate brown hair that rippled down her back. Right now Cecilia's pretty face was cold and scornful as she looked down her nose at Sam, arching one perfect sweep of an eyebrow.

'Hmmm, what do we have here?' drawled Cecilia, while her friends sniggered behind her. 'Ladies, it seems we are honoured to have the great Amy Grey's little sister on the yard. Come to

do Mummy and big sis proud, have we?'
Cecilia bent down and narrowed her eyes
at Sam. 'Be careful you don't fall off and
break your neck.' She straightened up,
flashing a cold smile. 'Good luck. We'll
all be watching you.'

Sam gazed after the slim back and the
bouncing chocolate curls as Cecilia and
her friends made their way to the outdoor
arena, the last dregs of her confidence
draining out through her feet.

'What a brat!' said a voice somewhere
by her knees. Startled, she looked
around but couldn't see anyone nearby.

The Shetlands had gathered near the gate again, chewing on their mouthfuls of hay, the crunch of their jaws loud in the barn.

Sam sighed and looked at her watch. Time to get her pony.

Chapter 2

Oscar was small, brown and white, and what Miss Mildew described as a 'pony with personality'. Sam thought he was a pain in the bum.

The second she took him out of the barn he stormed off at a trot for the water trough, despite the fact that he had water in the barn, dragging a helpless Sam along behind him. She hung onto his leather reins and tried to dig her heels into the concrete as Oscar put his ears back and hauled her along.

'For goodness sake child, *don't let him do that!*' shouted Miss Mildew from the centre of the arena where the rest of Sam's class were doing last-minute checks on their tack and getting onto their ponies' backs. Sam gritted her teeth and pulled hard on the reins but Oscar just waved his head in the air, a sulky expression on his face.

'If he bloats himself on water just before a lesson he will have terrible stomach ache,' ranted Miss Mildew, her eyes popping out of her head. 'That is a *terrible* way to treat one of *my* ponies!' Sam groaned as Oscar plunged his face into the water trough and let out a big snort, spraying water everywhere. *He isn't even thirsty!* she thought.

One of the older children took pity on her and helped her drag Oscar down to the arena where they pushed and pulled him through the gates to line up with the other ponies. Her face hot with embarrassment, Sam checked that the girth holding his saddle in place was nice and snug around his tummy so the saddle didn't slip when she got on. She put one foot in the stirrup and held on tight to Oscar's reins and the front of his saddle as she got ready to jump up. But as she put her weight on the stirrup and pushed off against the ground, Oscar stepped sideways, forcing her to hop after him. Her mouth went dry as she listened to the giggles coming from the arena wall where the older pupils had gathered to watch the lesson. She gritted her teeth,

waited for Oscar to stand still, and tried again. But as soon as she tried to jump up, he spun away again, his eyes shining with delight.

'Will you stop making such a fool of yourself and mount up, Samantha Grey. The entire class is waiting for you and we are now running five minutes late!' barked Miss Mildew.

'I'm trying, Miss Mildew,' panted Sam as her foot slipped from the stirrup and she bonked her nose on the saddle. Oscar span away again, prancing around her and obviously enjoying himself.

'Really!' exclaimed Miss Mildew as she strode over to Sam and Oscar, who froze as he saw her approach and tried to look innocent. 'This is not a good start and certainly not what I expect from you, Miss

Grey.' She tutted and grabbed the reins, holding Oscar firmly on the spot. 'Take a firm grip on those reins and mount up. Show him who is boss. If he has no respect for you, he will walk all over you!'

'Yes, Miss Mildew,' muttered Sam, as to her relief Oscar stood still and let her get on board. He trotted eagerly to the back of the ride and all the children walked their ponies around, nose to tail, waiting for their instructions.

It was a bit weird for Sam to be riding a little pony when she was so used to riding Velvet, who was after all, a proper horse. Velvet's long legs covered a lot more ground and her stride felt very smooth. Oscar pottered about on short legs and Sam struggled to get into the faster, choppier rhythm. Rising trot, something she could do easily on Velvet, was proving to be much harder on Oscar.

'Up, down, up, down, rise on your diagonals girls, grip with your thighs and lower leg, not your knees,' shouted Miss Mildew as they obediently trotted around the school. 'Can anyone tell me how to rise on the diagonal?'

'Yes, Ma'am,' said Natalie, a chubby girl with long brown plaits, whose family had recently moved over from New York.

'When the shoulder of the leg closest to the wall of the arena moves back towards you, you sit in the saddle, when it moves forwards you rise up again.'

'Well done, Natalie,' said Miss Mildew. 'So nice to see you were taught some proper riding in America after all.'

'Actually, English-style riding is quite popular in New York, Ma'am...' began Natalie.

'Thank you, my dear, I did not *actually* require an answer,' said Miss Mildew. 'Samantha, tell me why we rise to the trot.'

Sam bounced along and fumbled for a better grip on her reins while her mind searched for the answer. 'Rising to the trot frees up the horse's back and allows them to take longer, smoother strides, Miss Mildew. It also allows horse and rider to balance better.'

'Perhaps you could listen to your own answer then, Samantha, and not ride like a sack of potatoes.'

Sam flushed at the giggling from the sidelines and tried to relax her body into the saddle as Oscar jogged along.

For the next half hour all the pupils in the arena walked, trotted, and halted at the same time. Miss Mildew made them practise standing up in their stirrups in walk and trot to improve their balance. All of them wobbled and collapsed down into the saddle but none more so than Natalie, who couldn't seem to stand for more than a second. Sam was relaxing and beginning to enjoy herself until Miss Mildew decided they were all going to take it in turns to canter.

'On my command, you will each ride your ponies forward from trot to canter,' announced Miss Mildew. 'You will canter on the track until you get to the other end of the school where you will half halt and ride a 20-metre circle at a slower pace of canter before returning to the track and joining the back of the ride. Any questions?'

'What is half halt, Miss Mildew?' asked one of the girls.

'Half halt is when you squeeze gently on your pony's reins as if asking them to stop, while urging them on with your legs. This allows your animal to slow its pace, shorten its back, and balance better. It is *not* a signal to change pace. Your pony must continue on in canter. Begin.'

Sam gulped. She only knew how to canter in straight lines. She looked down

21

at Oscar and prayed he knew what he was doing.

Sam was relieved to see that no one in her class was able to do the circle perfectly. Some were egg-shaped, some were almost square, and some girls had problems keeping their ponies in canter at all. So when it came to her turn, she took a deep breath, asked Oscar to trot on and then sat down in the saddle, one leg on the girth, one leg behind it, and asked him to canter.

If Sam had been asked to describe what happened next, it would have been that Oscar decided to charge. He put his head down between his knees and shot forward at a gallop, pulling Sam over his neck as he tried to drag the reins from her hands. They were off the track by a mile and as they tore off to the other end of the arena,

Sam's breath caught in her throat and her body went light with fear. The air roared in her ears as they galloped past Miss Mildew. Sam could see Miss Mildew's narrow, sharp face screw up as she yelled, *'Sit up you silly girl!'*

Desperately, Sam tried to force her fear-rigid shoulders back, sit up straight, and keep her balance. The wall of the arena came closer at frightening speed and just as they were about to hit it, Sam managed to grab a couple of inches of rein and a fraction of control, enough to turn Oscar's head, and bank him in a sharp left.

I can do this, thought Sam, *I can do this*, as they headed for the corner she was supposed to turn out of to execute the circle. Oscar's body began to turn beneath her on the track as they hugged the wall and she sat back and asked for a half halt. His hoof beats slowed, his head came up, Sam grabbed a little bit more rein and thought, *YES, I'm DOING it*! as she tugged with the left hand and asked him to turn into a circle.

And then he did it again, head down, charging across the arena, dragging Sam down so close to his neck that she was practically kissing his mane. He was heading, not in a 20-metre circle, but in a straight line for Miss Mildew. Sam watched in horror as Miss Mildew's furious red face got closer and closer. She felt too helpless to stop Oscar but it didn't matter. Just before he ran over the owner of the riding school, he spun again, so quickly that Sam lost her balance and found herself somersaulting over his shoulder to land flat on her back

on the wood chip surface of the arena.

Sam gazed up at the blue sky above with serene fluffy white clouds scudding across it and tried to get some air working in her squished lungs. The fall had winded her quite badly. As she lay there gasping for air like a fish flopping on a riverbank, Miss Mildew's razor-sharp face, framed by a few strands of her straight black hair that had escaped from beneath her riding hat, slid into view. Her blue eyes were ice cold.

Sam gulped as she stared up at her.

'And what,' asked Miss Mildew, her voice a quiet hiss in the stunned silence, 'was that supposed to be, may I ask?'

Sam thought about it for a second. 'A ... brave ... attempt?' she wheezed.

Everyone burst out laughing, from the girls watching at the side of the arena to the girls sitting on their ponies in it. Miss Mildew didn't laugh. Her face just got redder, while her mouth got thinner and thinner as she pressed her lips into a hard white line.

'Get up, Miss Grey, and try to gain some control over your pony and a little over your mouth while you are at it.'

Wincing, Sam clambered to her feet and walked stiffly over to Oscar, who had rejoined the ride and was standing quietly, reins dangling and eyes sparkling. Sam gathered up the reins and heaved herself painfully into the saddle, coughing as her lungs sucked in air eagerly.

'Line up, everyone,' said Miss Mildew as the girls watching from the sidelines subsided into muffled giggles and whispers. Obediently, the whole class turned their ponies in until they all stood side by side in a neat line, facing Miss Mildew.

Miss Mildew glared down her sharp nose at them, both hands behind her back.

'Learning to become a horserider takes time, patience, courage, and hard work as well as natural talent,' she said. 'All of you are in this class because you have previous riding experience. All of you have parents or siblings that have already demonstrated an ability for the sport. I expect great things from this class and I certainly did not get them today.' She paused to glare at them as they all shifted nervously in their saddles.

'You are ambassadors for the sport and for this riding establishment,' continued Miss Mildew. 'You have eight weeks left until the end of term. A week after school breaks up, Meadow Vale will host its Summer Show . . . '

'*Nine weeks?!*' squeaked Natalie, white in the face. She cringed as Miss Mildew silenced her with a glare.

' . . . and you will all be entered as a matter of course. Think of the show as your end-of-term exam. I expect you all to work hard and improve *dramatically* over the coming weeks,' said Miss Mildew. 'Your names will go up on the office board this afternoon and you have until the end of the day to pick the pony you wish to compete on. You are dismissed.'

At that, Miss Mildew turned on her heel and marched out of the arena, not even pausing to glare at Natalie when she slid off her pony too fast and fell on her bottom.

Chapter 3

Sam sighed and started walking Oscar back up the yard. She could see the older girls drifting away from the arena wall, talking in low voices, and throwing amused glances over their shoulders at Sam's hot and bedraggled classmates. She looked for Amy but only got a glimpse of her bright pony tail as she strode off with her friends around a corner and out of sight. Sam's heart sank. She must have ridden really, really badly if Amy didn't even want to stick around to talk to her.

Oscar nearly stood on her foot in his eagerness to get back to a big feed of hay.

She felt like aiming a kick at his ample backside as she pulled the bridle off his face and watched him walk away into the cool interior of the barn.

'I won't be picking *you* for the show, that's for sure,' she said as she stuck her tongue out at him.

'Ooooh, he must be *sooooo* upset, not having a numptie like you want to ride him,' said a little voice dripping in sarcasm.

Startled, Sam looked around the barn but there was no one to be seen and, just like the last time, the voice seemed to be coming from somewhere around her knees. She looked down and saw one of the Shetlands, Apricot, looking up at her, her nose poking through the metal fences that divided the barn. There was no sign of anyone who could have spoken. She shook her head and went to put the saddle and bridle back into the tack room.

She ran to look in on her mother's mare, Velvet. The big black cob was still finishing her breakfast and was in no mood to come over to the stable door to say hello. Trailing her fingers against the wall, Sam walked down the row of stables. Lucy was back from her ride and in her stable cooling off.

The big piebald mare was always happy to have a face hug but as Sam reached up to cuddle her long nose, she turned around and backed her bum against the stable door.

'Be a love and give me tail a scratch would yer?'

Sam stood and stared at her, her jaw dropping so far it looked as if someone had unscrewed its hinges.

'Oooh, go on, just at the base of my tail, it don't half itch.'

'What's she up to, the silly old moo?' called a cheerful voice. Janey grinned at Sam and looked over her horse's door. 'Bless 'er, she just wants you to scratch her bum, Sam,' Janey laughed and dug her fingers in at the top of Lucy's tail, scratching hard. Lucy stretched her neck and groaned with pleasure.

'Yes,' said Sam. 'That's what she said.'

Janey looked at her with a smile. 'I know what you mean. Sometimes it does seem as if they talk, when you get to know their funny little ways.'

Dazed, Sam wandered away from Janey and out into the sunlight of the yard. She looked at the Shetlands' enclosure and there was Apricot, standing quite still by the gate, staring at her without blinking. She walked over slowly and crouched down so she was level with the mare's big brown eyes.

'Did you say something to me earlier today?' she asked in a whisper.

The little dappled brown mare snorted and shook her shaggy mane. 'Of course I did, you nitwit. What's surprising is that you heard me.'

Just then, a shadow fell across her and a small, black-booted foot kicked the gate. Sam flinched and wobbled, grabbing the bars to steady herself while Apricot backed off, snorting.

'Oh, I am *soooo* sorry, I seem to have done it again,' drawled Cecilia, as her friends giggled behind her. 'I just can't seem to stop walking all over you. Much like the ponies do. You really shouldn't keep getting in the way— insignificant little ants like you get trodden on.'

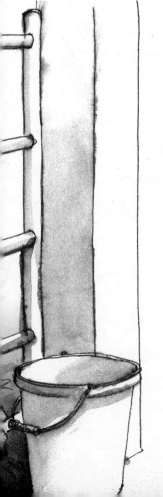

'Perhaps it's better she stay on the ground?' sneered Emma Crosby, a girl who fell just shy of pretty, with make-up pancaked on her face to disguise a rash of spots on her forehead and cheeks. 'The way she rides, it would be much safer and quicker just to lie down while the pony exercises itself around the arena.'

'What an excellent point, Emma,' said Cecilia, widening her eyes and nodding her head in mock admiration. 'We wouldn't want her getting hurt now, would we? And it would be so humiliating for our darling Amy to have to be the one with the stupid little sister who can't ride without falling off. Can you imagine how embarrassing it would be if she entered the show? Wouldn't you just *die* if she was your sister?'

Emma sneered while the rest of the coven laughed. 'Totally. After today's performance, I would have disowned her on the spot.'

'Absolutely,' said Cecilia. She flicked her eyes over Apricot and put her finger to her lips and frowned as she pretended to think really, really hard. 'Of course, you could always ride that little flea bag. You wouldn't have to worry about falling off because you could keep your feet on the ground while sitting in the saddle.' She leaned down and pinched Sam's cheek so hard, she yelped with pain. 'I really would think about it, sweetie. It's the only way you're going to make it through the show alive. See you around.' With that, Cecilia swept past, deliberately knocking into Sam as she did so. Emma and the rest of her friends followed in her wake, hips and shoulders jarring against Sam's skinny little body.

She watched them go with tears of anger and embarrassment pricking her eyes, her fingernails digging into her palms as she squeezed her hands into hard little fists.

'I hate her,' she hissed between clenched teeth. 'I really, really hate her.'

'Join the club,' said Apricot.

Sam looked down at her, still not ready to believe what her ears were hearing. 'What did you say?' she asked.

Apricot rolled her eyes. 'Give me strength,' she muttered. 'Deaf as well as thick—what a combination.' She raised her voice. 'I said, "Join the club".'

'What have you got against her?'

'A lot more than you,' said Apricot. 'Try having that spoilt little brat yanking on a piece of metal in your mouth and kicking you constantly in the ribs when she wants you to go faster.'

'She did that to you?' asked Sam.

'She did it to all of us,' said Turbo, a brown and white fuzzy Shetland, and so round he looked like a ball with tiny legs. 'She nearly gave me whiplash she yanked my head so hard to make me turn one day.'

'I'm still numb from the way she used to boot me around the arena,' said a Shetland called Mickey.

'All right, all right, I think she gets it!' yelled Apricot. 'I'm doing the talking here! The point is, we hate her, every pony on this yard that has had Cecilia Jones sitting on their backs hates her, like poison. But I've got an idea that will show up snobby knickers there and, between you and me, we'll make sure she gets what's coming to her.'

'OK,' said Sam. 'But can I just ask—why are you talking to me? Animals don't talk.'

Apricot ground her square teeth. 'Look, wally brain, it's dead simple. All animals can talk. It's just that half the time there's no point talking to two legs. Very few of you bother to really listen to animals when they talk and those that do, well, most of them start gibbering and frothing at the mouth, and saying they need a lie down in a dark room. But you seem to be able to hear us well enough—you just need to get your brain used to the idea that we can talk. If you're going to turn into a gibberer, I'd do it now. Save us both a lot of bother.'

Sam looked back at Apricot and thought, *This is the maddest thing I have ever done. I must have knocked my head harder than I thought when I fell off Oscar.* 'Fine,' she said. 'What's the plan?'

Apricot squealed with delight and reared up on her little legs as the other Shetlands gathered around. 'Excellent!' she whinnied.

'We watched your lesson today . . . '

Sam groaned.

'It wasn't that bad, young 'un, it really wasn't,' said Turbo kindly.

'It wasn't great either,' said Apricot. 'But there is no reason why you wouldn't put in a decent performance at the Meadow Vale Show if you practised really hard over the next nine weeks.'

'But I had no control!' wailed Sam. 'It was awful. I thought I was going to puke or break my neck, or both!'

'That was nothing to do with you. Oscar's always a bit mental when he's had a

43

break,' said Turbo.

'Oi!' said Oscar, popping his head up from the other side of the fence, hay sticking out of his mouth.

'Oh please, for the first lesson after every school holiday you are always a pain in the neck,' said Apricot. 'Give it a rest! Getting back to the *point* of this conversation, you could easily put on a decent performance at the show. The basics are there, you just need a bit of confidence and a bit of practise. But if you really want to get at Miss Snobby Knickers, that's not enough.'

'Why not?' asked Sam.

'Because you have to be better than her,' said Apricot.

'She's older than me, more experienced than me,' pointed out Sam. 'I'm not going to get better than her in just nine weeks.'

'No, not in terms of skill, you're not,' said Apricot.

'Then how?' said Sam.

'If you really want to get your own back on Cecilia Jones, then you have got to do something she can't,' said Apricot. 'You've got to enter the show and do well on a pony she can't ride. All that takes is a bit of guts.'

Sam stared at Apricot, who looked, now that she really thought about it, a little bit nuts. But then all Shetlands seemed to have that irritated, eyes-going-in-two-different-directions, loopy look on their faces. She thought of Cecilia riding, how cool and confident she always seemed, how *terrified* she was of the fiery ponies Cecilia always seemed to prefer.

She swallowed, her mouth dry. 'Who?'

Apricot curled her top lip back over her nose and grinned. 'Mulberry. If you want to shoot to the top of the herd on this yard and grind Cecilia's face in the dust in nine weeks, you've got to ride Mulberry.'

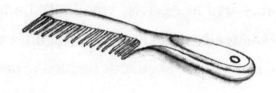

Chapter 4

The barn went so quiet, Sam could have heard a pin drop. Oscar even stopped chewing for a second and looked at Apricot with his eyes bulging out of his head in surprise. He muttered, 'Mental!' under his breath and ducked out of sight. The rest of the Shetlands just stared at Apricot who had a triumphant, *Aren't-I-fantastic?* look on her face. Sam was half expecting her to do the splits on her back legs, fling her front hoofs up in the air and shout, 'Ta daaaaa!'

'Brilliant!' said Turbo at last. 'Pure bloomin' genius.'

'Thank you very much,' said Apricot, bowing and scraping. 'I'm 'ere all week.'

'Who on earth is Mulberry?' asked Sam, as the Shetlands bounced up and down and squealed with delight.

'I'll tell you who she is,' said a deep, slow voice, that trickled through her ears like warm honey. Basil, a huge cob in the next section of the barn, swung his head around and looked at her over his huge bottom with his sleepy eyes. 'She's the pony Miss Mildew has had to retire from the riding school for injuring so many riders. She's old and very, very grumpy. She kicks, she bucks, she rears, and she bites. In short, she's not the one for you.

Cecilia Jones will get her comeuppance one of these days, and you won't have to break your neck to make sure it happens.'

'She's not that bad!' exclaimed Apricot.

'No?' asked Basil. 'Why don't you tell the little two-legs here some of Mulberry's nicknames?'

'Pfffftttt,' said Apricot rudely, as she blew a huge raspberry at Basil. 'What's in a name? I don't see what that's got to do with anything . . .'

'Pocket Rocket,' said Basil, as he swung his huge body around to face Apricot. 'Tasmanian Devil, Grumpy Knickers, Buckaroo, and my personal favourite . . .'

'Don't say it!' warned Apricot.

'Walking Evil,' said Basil.

Sam closed her eyes as the yard spun around her.

'Don't listen to him! We can help you,' said Apricot. 'Mulberry isn't that bad when you get to know her and you—'

Sam opened her eyes to see Apricot staring up at her, eyes shining.

'You can talk to her, get into her head,' breathed Apricot. 'I'll bet she's never had a rider that can do that!'

'Why would the little two-legs want to do that?' asked Basil. 'Five minutes in Mulberry's company is enough to give you nightmares at the thought of what's floating around in her head.'

'Shut up, shut up, *shut up*!' screamed Apricot. 'You're spoiling my plan, you great big slow-brained cob. And get away from the fence!'

Basil cocked his head and looked down his long nose at Apricot, a sly twinkle in his eye. 'What, this fence?' he asked, all innocence. He took a careful step forward, his shadow falling across the Shetland. 'You want me not to get too close to *this* fence?'

Apricot ground her teeth and Sam could see her mane shaking with rage. Turbo and Mickey jittered around her, trying to calm her down. 'Just blank it all out, think

soothing thoughts. You're in the zone, you are the zone, and the zone is you . . . '

But it was no use. Apricot lost her temper and charged Basil, rearing up to snap at his face just as he pulled his head up, before she turned around and kicked out with both hind legs, screeching with rage.

Sam backed away as Basil laughed and taunted Apricot, while Mickey and Turbo tried to calm her down. Oscar was right. The Shetlands were totally mental.

Sam wandered down to the outdoor arena to watch some of the older girls practise their jumping. She sighed as she watched them glide over the ground and over jumps, ponies sure-footed and, above all, *obedient*. A horse-shaped shadow fell across her and she felt a warm hand on her shoulder.

She looked up into Amy's eyes, green mirrors of her own. She was dressed for riding and was holding Velvet's reins in one hand. The big black mare rumbled a greeting in her throat and nuzzled Sam with her soft nose.

Sam smiled and stroked the mare's face. 'Where did you go after my lesson?' she asked Amy.

Amy pulled a face. 'I still had mucking out to do and I didn't want Miss Mildew to think I was slacking off. I had to leg it down to the bottom yard before she got there.'

'Oh,' said Sam. 'It wasn't . . . wasn't,' she was horrified to feel a hot blush stealing over her cheeks. 'It wasn't because of the way I rode.'

Amy giggled and tweaked a piece of Sam's

hair. 'Don't be silly, you little monkey. You didn't exactly turn out an award-winning performance but Oscar's always a bit of a pain in the bum when he's had a break.' Amy hooked her foot into a stirrup and sprang lightly into the saddle. She grinned down at Sam. 'Besides, not everyone can be as fabulous as me!' She clicked her tongue and urged Velvet into a walk.

Sam clenched and unclenched her fists by her sides as she watched her sister ride Velvet around the arena, the mare bouncing lightly on her hoofs, neck arched, muscles bunching beneath a black coat that shone with ripples of light. Amy had been joking, she knew that. Amy was a good, kind, thoughtful big sister who always protected her. But it would be nice, just once, if she could be the one who impressed Amy.

Frowning, Sam walked slowly to the office and peeked through the glass door to make sure no one was inside. She walked to the reception desk and picked up the clipboard with the list of names of pupils entered for the Meadow Vale show. Some pupils had already scribbled down the names of the animals they wanted to ride. Sam picked up a pencil and chewed on it thoughtfully, staring at the blank box next to her name. Then she quickly scribbled a name, threw the clipboard down, and ran from the office before anyone could catch her, her tummy pricking with fear and glee.

As she dodged around riders and horses, she could see in her mind's eye the list and the name she had written next to hers.

Mulberry.

Chapter 5

Miss Mildew was waiting for them when they got to the yard the next day. Her face had turned so red, it looked like it was going to explode, and splatter in all directions like an overripe tomato.

Sam saw her storming towards them with the clipboard as she, Mum, and Amy got out of the car. Sam tried to shrink so that she could hide behind Amy as Miss Mildew strode up to them.

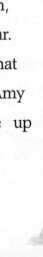

'Is this a joke?' she demanded as she showed Mum the list. 'Because if this is your idea of funny, Samantha Grey, I'm not laughing.'

Sam watched Mum scan the list, puzzled, and she cringed at the frown that puckered between her eyes when she read the name next to Sam's. She glanced at Amy, her eyes angry. 'Did you put Sam up to this?'

'Put her up to what?' asked Amy. 'I don't know what you're talking about, honest.'

Without a word, Mum passed Amy the clipboard and Sam watched the same expressions on Amy's face as she read the name. This really was embarrassing. Sam had decided the whole Mulberry thing was a bad idea and she had hardly slept a wink last night, wondering if they got to the yard early enough, whether she would be able to rub the name out. Too late now.

'Sam, did Cecilia suggest you ride this pony?' Amy asked.

'No!' squeaked Sam. 'I'm not stupid.'

'You must be, to ask for *this* pony,' said Miss Mildew, her voice shaking with anger.

Suddenly, Miss Mildew had that funny look on her face that told Sam she knew she had said the wrong thing but was hoping no one would notice. No chance— Mum had ears like a bat and she never, ever let anything go. It was one of the things that drove Sam crazy about her. Mum glared at Miss Mildew and drew herself up so she was looking down her nose at her. 'I suggest we go to the office to discuss this, before you forget yourself altogether, Miss Mildew.'

A little of the colour went from Miss Mildew's face. She nodded curtly and marched ahead of them into the office. Mum gave Sam *That Look* before walking after her, Amy and Sam trailing in her wake.

'First of all, I do not like anyone calling either of my daughters stupid, regardless of their actions,' said Mum, in a cool tone

of voice. Sam hovered nervously by the door in case she needed a quick getaway and Amy threw herself into the nearest chair, flicking her fringe out of her eyes. 'I am sure she has a good reason to pick Mulberry—or else someone on this yard has misled her.'

Miss Mildew nodded and turned to glare at Sam. 'Please explain to your mother and myself why you picked this pony, of all the animals on this yard. Did someone tell you to ride her?'

Sam thought of her conversation with Apricot yesterday in the barn. She looked at Miss Mildew and Mum and decided that neither of them were ready for the news that Apricot could not only talk, but was possibly a budding evil genius with plans for world domination.

She took a deep breath. 'Not exactly,' she said. 'I just heard that Mulberry was a very good pony that was not being used very much these days.'

'And do you know *why* she isn't being used?' demanded Miss Mildew.

'Um, because she's a bit stroppy and some of the beginners had problems with her?' offered Sam.

'A bit stroppy?' said Miss Mildew in utter disbelief. '*A bit stroppy with the beginners?*' She turned back to Mum. 'She cannot ride that animal, it will be a disaster.'

Mum looked at Sam thoughtfully as she pulled on her leather riding gloves. Sam widened her eyes as she stared back at her, willing her mother to give her a chance, to be as confident in her as she was in Amy.

'It might not be a disaster, Miss Mildew,'

said Mum. 'Sam is correct—Mulberry is difficult, not unrideable, and neither of my daughters are novices.'

'Cecilia Jones couldn't ride her . . . ' said Miss Mildew.

'But Amy could,' Mum interrupted. Inside her head, Sam groaned. Amy *could* ride Mulberry, which meant Sam *had* to, or she would never live it down. Apricot had kept that bit of information to herself. Sam imagined her giggling away to herself like a lunatic in the barn.

'Not every pony goes well for every rider,' continued Mum. 'Just because Cecilia Jones could not ride Mulberry, does not mean that Sam cannot. If she thinks she can do it, then I have every confidence in my daughter.'

Mum looked at her, her expression

unreadable, but Sam knew what she was asking. *Do you think you can ride Mulberry, Sam? Do you have faith in yourself?*

Sam swallowed. She was glad Mum was not asking the question out loud.

'She will need lots of lessons if she wants to get to grips with that mare before the show,' said Miss Mildew. Sam swore she looked almost cheerful at the thought of getting more money out of Mum.

'Of course,' said Mum. 'But as Mulberry is not being used in the riding school at the moment, Sam can ride her as often as she likes between now and the show. I understand Mulberry is up for sale so if Sam can make her look good, it will only increase her price.'

Miss Mildew looked at Mum with her eyes narrowed for a moment and then nodded her head.

'She might as well get started now,' said Miss Mildew. She walked quickly to the door with her jerky, angry stride, and yanked it open. 'Janey!' she shouted, not looking at all her prim and proper self. As Janey came bustling up, her curly brown hair working itself free from its pony tail, Miss Mildew jerked her head in Sam's direction. 'Samantha Grey has decided to ride Mulberry at the Summer Show. Please introduce them and give her a lesson.'

That was it. Fight over. Miss Mildew simply stalked off and left Janey staring at Sam with her mouth open.

'Bless you,' said Janey. 'Been taking your brave pills, have you?'

Mum wrapped her arms around Sam's skinny shoulders. 'Looks like it,' she said, smiling down at her. Sam could smell that delicious mix of horse and leather polish coming from Mum's riding clothes and the chocolatey scent of cocoa butter that she rubbed into her skin. She wanted to confess everything right there and then; that she didn't want to ride Mulberry, that there were days she didn't want to ride at

all, that she would never, ever be Amy.

'If you want to back out of this, Sam, and ride another pony, that's fine,' said Mum, the corner of her eyes crinkling with a kind smile. 'There's no shame in it.'

Sam opened her mouth to say something and then she saw Amy over Mum's shoulder, looking at her with the same kind, crinkle-eyed smile. Sam closed her lips with a snap and just shook her head.

Mum looked worried for a moment and then gave her a gentle push. 'Off you go then. Be good . . . '

' . . . work hard, have fun.' Sam finished the sentence she heard every school morning. She smiled at them both and turned to walk after Janey.

Janey whistled cheerfully and called out hellos to liveries and workers as they made their way down to the little square of stables where Miss Mildew kept her own horses and any animals that were ill or being sold. It was quiet and peaceful on the bottom yard and only Miss Mildew's favourite helpers were allowed down here to care for the animals. Helpers like Cecilia Jones.

'Is Mulberry really as bad as everyone says?' asked Sam.

'Depends,' said Janey. 'She's a bit like Marmite, is our Mulberry. You either love her or you hate her. Personally, I've always got on with her.'

All the stables on the bottom yard faced inward, and it was half-roofed against the sky. Sam walked after Janey through an open doorway and found herself standing on sacred ground.

The bottom yard was cool and quiet. There was none of the noise and bustle of the top yard or the barns where riding school horses, students, and helpers scurried to and fro. Here was peace and sunlight dancing on flagstones. There was the odd snort, the sound of munching as Miss Mildew's gleaming horses dozed in their stables. Sam winced at the ringing sound Janey's riding boots made against the stone as she strode across the yard to a stable tucked into the farthest corner, with no name on the door. 'Come say hello then!' said Janey.

Sam tiptoed nervously to the door, her cool fingers wrapping over the top of it, rough wood nibbling her skin. The stable was dark, the sun blocked by the half roof. She squinted into the gloom, thinking at first that Janey was joking and the stable was empty, until a patch of pure black shifted at the back wall and she caught a glimpse of white as the pony rolled its eye at her.

It was an effort to make anything out, but from what she could see, Mulberry was a pretty pony, with a short, strong back, slender legs, an arched neck, and an elegant head. Her coat was jet black and her mane and tail were thick and bushy. Sam held out a hand and clicked her tongue at the mare. 'Come here and let me see you girl,' she cooed.

She screamed as the mare shot forward, teeth bared, and she jumped back so quickly she lost her balance and sat down hard on the floor, bruising her bum. Janey laughed as the mare pulled ugly faces at

Sam over the stable door, snapping her teeth, eyes narrowed to slits. She scratched the angry little pony behind the ear.

'Told you,' Janey grinned. 'Marmite.'

Chapter 6

After ten minutes of struggling to get Mulberry to stand still and not threaten to kick or bite when being groomed and tacked with a saddle and bridle, Sam decided she had been an absolute fool for ever listening to Apricot, that selfish, revenge-mad Shetland.

She didn't get a chance to talk to Mulberry because Janey stood with her the whole time, showing her how to slip the bridle on over Mulberry's head, guide the bit between her snapping teeth, slip the saddle down her back, and do up the girth while dodging Mulberry's flashing

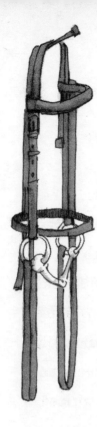

hoofs. She knew Janey meant well but she needed to talk to Mulberry and get her to calm down, before she did her some damage.

Finally, Mulberry was tacked up and ready for her lesson. The little mare was so aggressive that Sam could feel those tiny reserves of courage trickle right out through her feet. She felt sick at the thought of riding Mulberry—if she behaved so badly on the ground, what on earth was she going to do to her when she got on her back? Her fingers shook as she pushed the straps on the bridle into the little leather loops—keepers—that stopped them flapping around.

'Ready then?' asked Janey.

No, thought Sam. But, feeling quite numb by now, she simply grabbed Mulberry's reins and tried to walk her up to the outdoor school.

Mum had always taught her never to hit a pony or to lose her temper with one, but Mulberry was behaving like an idiot and Sam could have happily slapped her as she tried to drag her along the yard. Mulberry bounced about on her hard little blue hoofs, snorting and prancing. A car door slammed and she jumped forward and then spun around, dragging Sam with her. She felt as if her arm was being slowly wrenched from its socket as she pulled on the reins and fought to get Mulberry to walk quietly by her side.

'What a silly thing she is,' tutted Janey,

as Mulberry jittered and jogged. 'Never mind, she'll settle once you start working her. Hasn't been ridden for nearly six months now, mind. She's bound to be a little bit fresh.'

'How fresh?' squeaked Sam, red in the face and panting with effort, as Mulberry spun again.

Janey laughed and grabbed the reins on the other side, helping Sam to steady the snorting pony. 'Fresh enough that she won't be boring to ride, but don't you go looking at me with those big puppy eyes—I wouldn't put you up on her if I didn't think you could get a tune from her. She's a good pony, is this one, if you can just click with her.'

Like Amy did, thought Sam miserably as Mulberry dragged them past the barn.

Apricot stood by the gate, brown eyes gleaming. Basil just shook his long face and carried on eating his hay.

They managed to get Mulberry into the middle of the school and she stood quietly enough, looking around her with wary eyes.

'Bless her!' said Janey. 'I bet she's forgotten what the school is for.'

Janey held Mulberry still while Sam got her foot into the stirrup and scrambled aboard. It was not the most elegant mount up and Mulberry shook her head in irritation and snapped her teeth. Luckily, it was still early in the morning and everyone was so busy mucking out and feeding breakfasts that

they did not have time to come down to the arena and watch the lesson.

At first Mulberry seemed a bit dull. She was slow to start working and Sam felt like getting off her and pushing her into a trot, like an old car that was having trouble starting. But as Janey shouted instructions and Sam began to feel a little bit more confident, Mulberry began to snort and jog around the arena. She kept jumping with fear every time a car passed, bending her body to get away from the arena wall and fighting Sam for the reins. As the fear began to build in her belly, Sam could feel herself losing her position and this made her panic even more.

Riding is not about hanging on, it's about balance, she heard Mum say. *Keep your balance and you will stick to the saddle like glue.*

But Sam was tensing up and she could feel herself leaning forward. She tried not to curl up in the saddle, as she knew that would throw her off balance and make it much easier for her to fall off. Her hands gripped the reins so hard, her knuckles were turning white and her toes began

to dip downwards, the stirrups sliding to the back of her heel, instead of resting on the ball of her foot. She was not a rider at the moment, she was just a passenger, clinging on in an ever more dangerous position. She had a nasty feeling that Mulberry knew that.

'Sit up, Sam, shoulders back, toes up!' called Janey. Sam took deep breaths to steady her nerves and forced her body to relax.

'At the next corner I want you to sit up, lean back slightly, sit deep into the saddle, and ask for canter,' said Janey.

As Mulberry jogged along at an uncomfortable speed, Sam watched the corner rush towards her.

'I can't do it!' she gasped.

'Yes, you can!' said Janey. 'It's nothing

you haven't done a million times before, you'll be fine.'

'She'll go mad!' said Sam, as Mulberry tensed up beneath her and began to feel more like an unexploded bomb waiting to go off than a pony.

'She'll be fine,' said Janey. 'Just sit deep into the saddle, get a good position, and ride her forward confidently. She might be a bit rusty but she knows her job.'

But Sam's courage deserted her and Mulberry jogged through the corner rather faster than Sam felt they should in trot.

'OK, I want you to think positively and at the next corner I want you to sit up and kick on,' said Janey.

'I can't do it!' wailed Sam.

'Yes, you can,' said Janey. 'You have to

believe that you can.'

The corner loomed and then fell behind them as Mulberry and Sam trotted on.

'OK, the next corner, we are definitely going to do this at the next corner,' said Janey. 'Think really hard about what you want her to do, ask her loud and clear, and then ride her like you stole her!'

As the next corner rushed to meet them, Sam took a really deep breath, sat down in the saddle, and asked for canter.

Mulberry bounded lightly into the faster pace, a little too fast for Sam's liking. She did a half halt without thinking, drawing the reins through her hands for a stronger hold, squeezing with her legs, and her heart soared when the little black mare responded. They cantered around the arena at a steady pace, Mulberry's neck arched so she looked as pretty as a fairy tale horse, while Janey shouted encouragement. Mulberry was lovely to ride; fast, powerful, but quick to respond to a twitch on the reins. Sam began to grin from ear to ear as they cantered down the long side of the arena. Six more weeks of this and they were going to clean up at the show! Everyone was going to have to admit that she was a good rider, as good as Amy, better than Cecilia!

And then it all went wrong.

Mulberry tried to slow down as they rode past the gate, but Sam squeezed her sides with her legs, the signal to keep going. As soon as she did this, Mulberry locked her legs, ploughing up the wood chip of the arena as she skidded to a stop, throwing a stunned Sam over her shoulder so sharply

she turned over in the air before landing
on her back for the second time that week.

Dull pain blossomed in her back and
skull, and Sam was grateful that Mum
insisted she wear a body protector as well
as a hard hat when she rode. Mulberry
walked over to peer into her face and then

shook her mane and trotted over to the
gate. Sam was convinced she heard an evil
little snigger.

Janey walked over to help her up and
dusted her off as Sam tried to cough up
a bit of wood chip that had lodged in her
throat.

'That,' said Janey, 'was Mulberry's famous Sliding Stop. Easy enough to sit to if you lean back but the trick is to keep her busy so she doesn't have time to think of nasty things to do to you. But we'll work on that in the next lesson.'

'Oh great' said Sam weakly. 'I can't wait.'

Chapter 7

Mulberry, it turned out, had a lot of tricks up her sleeve. As well as her world famous Sliding Stop, there was her Jack Knife, when she sprang forward and twisted her body at an angle, the Stop and Spin, where she hit the brakes hard and then spun to the right, dropping her shoulder as she did so, or the Wall of Death, which was when she charged round and round the arena at flat out gallop, with Sam clinging onto her neck for dear life.

Sam and Mulberry were having two lessons a week with Janey and on top of that she sneaked Mulberry down to the outdoor arena as often as she could to practise on her own. She was getting better—at least, she was not falling off as much. But Mulberry still wasn't listening to her.

Even worse, she wasn't talking to her either. Sam spoke to the mare every chance she could get, whispering in her ear when she was grooming her and tacking her up, talking to her in the arena as they rode. But although Mulberry flicked an ear in her direction and sometimes cocked her head and listened with her black eyes gleaming, she did not say a word in reply.

The whole yard knew now that she was riding Mulberry in the Summer Show, so every time she led Mulberry from her stable, tack jingling softly, she seemed to have an audience waiting for her. They lined up at the side wall of the arena and Sam could feel her fingers grow thick and clumsy under their watching eyes.

Of course, Cecilia Jones and her vile friends always had fun mocking Sam and the way she rode. They didn't dare do it if Amy was there, but the rest of the time Sam had to endure nasty little comments said in quiet voices so the adults couldn't hear as she passed them at the wall. Some of the girls tried to be helpful and tell her how to ride Mulberry but progress was very, very slow. With just four weeks to go to the Summer Show, Sam felt no more confident than she did the first day she rode Mulberry.

'Why on earth did you pick Mulberry?' asked Amy one day, when Sam took another tumble in canter.

'Because I want to be a good rider,' puffed Sam as they chased Mulberry around the arena.

'But you are a good rider,' said Amy.

'Do you really think so?' said Sam.

'Of course I do, you little monkey!' laughed Amy, as she grabbed Mulberry's reins and pulled her to a stop. 'So does Mum. But you have to believe you are a good rider and stop beating yourself up.'

'I get scared,' said Sam, in a small voice. 'And it all goes wrong. I lean forward and I stop thinking and then I fall off.'

'We all get scared,' said Amy, tweaking a lock of Sam's hair and smiling gently. 'Everyone gets scared, even the great Miss Mildew. It's not nice when things are going wrong. But you have to trust yourself and trust your pony and just ride through the fear. Remember what Mum always says? *When you get into trouble . . . '*

' . . . kick on,' said Sam, grinning. Amy laughed.

'But seriously, why Mulberry?' asked Amy. 'She's a nightmare at the best of times. She had me off more times than I could count.'

'Really? You?' asked Sam, unable to believe that her amazing big sister ever struggled with anything.

'Sam, Mulberry throws *everyone!'* laughed Amy. 'Cecilia wouldn't ride her because she didn't make her look good. She's really hard work and I see you down here, sweating and puffing and white in the face with nerves, trying to get her to behave and go nicely. So why keep doing it?'

Sam thought for a moment. She thought about Cecilia Jones, the show, Amy, all the reasons she told herself why she stuck it out with Mulberry day after day. Then she thought about what *really* made her get back on after every fall. She smiled.

'When I ride the riding school ponies I

feel safe,' she said. 'But they are so hard to get going and they feel a bit dull to ride. When I ride Mulberry, when things go right, she's so quick and fast. It's like my legs melt into her and we turn and move together. It's like . . . like . . . '

'Flying,' said Amy, her eyes misty as she stroked Mulberry's neck. 'It's like flying.' She smiled at Sam. 'I remember now. Well, you'd better get back on and have another go if you want to be ready for the show.'

Sam groaned and gathered up her reins.

But one hot summer afternoon, with just three weeks to go to the show, after another ride in the arena where Mulberry had managed to catapult her through the air again, Sam was beginning to doubt she would ever fly. Bruised, battered, and exhausted, she let Mulberry back into her stable, locked the door, and staggered away from the bottom yard, her eyes blurred with tears. The yard lay sleeping under the hot, heavy air. Stabled horses dozed with their noses on their chest and any spare humans had found somewhere quiet and shady, away from the sun.

Her shoulder aching from another slam dunk into the wood chip surface of the arena, she trudged through the sleepy yard to Velvet's stable. It was cool and dark and dust motes danced in the shafts of bright sunlight that penetrated tiny holes in the corrugated iron roof. The smell of clean straw tickled Sam's nose and the only noise was the steady munch of Velvet's jaws as she chewed on her hay and the swish of her tail as she flicked a stray fly from her hindquarters.

Sam pulled back the bolt on the door and slipped into the stable. She laid her head against Velvet's shoulder and gazed up at her face but the big mare just flicked her ears back in Sam's direction and carried on eating.

'I can't do this,' she whispered. 'I'm tired and I'm sore and most of all, I'm terrified. That pony is a raving nutcase and there is no way I can ride her in the show.' Hot tears began to slip down her cheeks. 'You're the only one I ever felt safe on and you never talk to me! You never say a word to me and it's not fair!'

Velvet stopped munching and swung her head around to look at Sam. 'But you know I love you?' she asked in a sweet, soft voice.

Sam's breath caught in her throat. 'Yes,' she whispered.

'Then what more is there to say?' said Velvet.

Sam stepped forward until she was under Velvet's jaw and the mare bent her head and sniffed her face all over, as she had always done since Sam was tiny, the whiskers on her mouth brushing her skin with little feather touches, her nostrils flaring as she pulled in the scent of Sam, the sweet smell of hay on her breath washing over Sam's face. Then she leaned down and pulled Sam back against her chest with her head and held her there while Sam cried into Velvet's satin skin.

Later that day, Sam walked over to the barn and looked in on the Shetlands. Apricot looked up from where she was snoozing on her feet and wandered over. Turbo and Mickey both lay flat out in the straw, snoring gently.

'I'm not doing so well,' Sam whispered.

'I can see that,' said Apricot, snorting through her huge nostrils. 'Swallow any more wood chip and Mildew is going to charge you for a new surface. Get on with it—you've only got three weeks to go!'

'I know!' said Sam. 'But it's not that simple. Mulberry won't talk to me.' A nasty thought dawned on her. 'Mulberry can talk, can't she?'

'Course she can!' snarled Apricot. 'Don't you start that "animals can't talk" rubbish with me. I've heard Mulberry talk plenty

of times and a right gob she has on her an'
all.'

'But she never says a word to me!' said
Sam.

'Then you aren't talking to her right,'
said Apricot.

'What?'

'Give me strength, you nit-witted, flea-
addled, little two-legs,' snarled Apricot.
'We're not like you lot. We don't go around
talking just for the sake of it, we have to
have something we think is worth saying.
Whatever you're spouting at Mulberry,
she obviously thinks it's drivel, which is
why she isn't talking back. Or listening to
it either, I bet.'

'Well, what am I supposed to say then?'
asked Sam.

'How should I know? You're meant to

be the smart one with thumbs and all the tool-using skills. Think of something, you skinny ape!'

'You are so rude!'

'Rather be rude than stupid,' said Apricot. 'All this time trying to get to grips with Walking Evil and you *still* haven't found what makes her tick. What have you been talking about?'

'I've just been telling her about my day, how much I like her, how pretty she is . . . ' Sam stuttered into silence as Apricot put her head back and roared with laughter.

'You're trying to get her to *like* you?' wheezed Apricot. 'Are you going to braid her mane with pretty ickle ribbons and be bestest friends?'

'All right then smarty pants,' hissed Sam, her face hot with embarrassment, as Apricot subsided into giggles. 'If you want your revenge on Cecilia you'd better start telling me everything you know about Mulberry.'

Apricot thought about it for a minute and then shrugged. 'Not much to tell. She hates you lot—young 'uns bring her out in a rash, so it's pointless asking her to be nice—and she wishes she could go back to being a driving pony. That's about it.'

'When was Mulberry a driving pony?'

'Oooh, years ago, before she came to Meadow Vale. The last two-legs that owned her was old and they used to enter her into competitions, pulling a fancy little carriage with them sitting in like Lord and Lady Muck. She used to bang on and on about it, how she always won rosettes, the time she brought a trophy home, blah, blah, blah, blah . . . '

'Did she now?' said Sam, as a light-bulb moment lit up her brain. 'Apricot, how good is your acting?'

Chapter 8

Mulberry did not want to talk, as usual. As soon as she saw Sam's face appear over the stable door she turned to face the wall, presenting Sam with her rather big bum. Sam smiled and quickly pulled a serious face as Mulberry glanced at her over her shoulder.

'It's OK Mulberry, I'm not going to try and talk to you any more,' she said in a soft voice. 'I know you don't really like me and its pointless me entering the show with you as my pony. It's a lot of hassle and you're not really bothered.' Sam began to walk away as Mulberry turned to face her with her ears pricked forward. 'I'll just do what Apricot said and pick one of the fancier show ponies. She did warn me that you wouldn't be up to competing any more.'

'Apricot said *what*?' hissed a harsh voice behind her. Sam allowed herself a quick grin before turning slowly back to the stable door. Mulberry had her head hanging over the half door, her eyes slitted with anger and her ears pinned right back against her head.

'Oh, so you do talk,' said Sam.

'What. Did. Apricot. Say?' asked Mulberry, spitting the words out between her grinding teeth.

'Well, I don't want to cause any trouble . . . '

'TELL ME!' neighed Mulberry.

'OK, OK!' said Sam. 'She basically said

that it's been ages since you did a show, and seeing as your heart isn't really in it your days of competing against better ponies and winning are long gone. And that I should pick something else if I want to look good on the day.'

'There isn't an animal on this yard that could make you look good when you ride, you graceless lump,' snarled Mulberry.

Sam shrugged. 'Whatever. I'm going to do what Apricot says and pick a different pony. So you're off the hook.'

'That cheeky, bad-mannered madam of a Shetland,' roared Mulberry. 'Let me out, two-legs!'

'Why?'

'Let me out, put me on a bloomin' lead rope and get me up to that barn! I can't walk up there myself; they'll think I'm escaping and I want a word with that runt,' said Mulberry.

Sam clipped a lead rope onto Mulberry's head collar and opened the stable door. Mulberry nearly wrenched Sam's aching shoulder from its socket as she marched

out of the stable and through the yard,
dragging Sam in her wake. They got a
few funny looks from passing riders and
staff as Sam struggled to catch up with
Mulberry and look as if she was leading
her. Mulberry did not pay her the slightest

bit of attention—she was far too busy muttering angrily under her breath.

She stomped to a halt outside the Shetland's gate and glared at Apricot, who lidded her eyes and looked bored.

'Come here, you little pot-bellied, hippo-faced sack of manure!' snarled Mulberry. Sam saw Turbo open one eye where he lay dozing in the straw and then shut it again quickly. One ear flicked up, though, and swivelled in Mulberry's direction.

'What's your problem?' yawned Apricot.

'You know full well what my problem is!' screeched Mulberry. 'Where do you get off telling this little two-legs, who can't ride for toffee, that I'm not up to competing any more?'

Apricot shrugged. 'Well, aren't you?' she asked.

'No, I am bloomin' well not!' exploded Mulberry. 'Who do you think you are? When have you ever competed, eh? You've not been off this yard in your whole life. You've played nursemaid to babies while I've been competing at local and national level, winning a prize in every competition, bringing home cups . . . '

'Blah, blah, blah, blah, BLAH!' said Apricot. 'You *used* to do all that, Miss High and Mighty, Miss I'm-better-than-the-whole-yard-put-together, but you don't do it any more, do you? Your glory days are well behind you and now you're neither use nor ornament. I may not be a world traveller like yourself but at least I can be trusted with a rider on my back, which is more than can be said for you, your Majesty. Sittin' around here all day long, eating your head off, and not doing a stroke of work!'

Mulberry bared her teeth and shook her mane. 'You're just jealous, because I get to live as I please.'

'Oh, jealous, is it?' shot back Apricot. 'If you think that, then you've lost any brains you might have had. I might as well start packing your things.'

'What are you on about now?' snapped Mulberry.

'Think about it. You won't let anyone

ride you and you're down on the bottom yard 'cause Mildew wants to sell you. But if you don't put on a good performance at the show, who is going to buy a child's pony that can't be ridden? Do you really think Mildew is going to keep feeding you for free?'

There was a snigger from Turbo's direction and a soft voice said, 'Good night, God bless, don't let the door hit your bum on the way out.'

Mulberry looked horrified. 'She wouldn't dare!'

'Oh, wouldn't she?' asked Apricot. 'I dunno, perhaps you've got a "special" relationship with her and she'll let you do your own thing, at her expense, for a long, long time. Or *maybe* she'll sell you to the first numpties that come along just to be rid of you? Maybe she won't even check that they can offer you a good home, a warm stable, lots to eat? Maybe she'll let them dump you in a field to live out your life in all weathers with screeching little two-legs telling you to giddy up all day along and thwacking you with whips? Whaddya think?'

Mulberry looked at Apricot for a long moment and then turned on her fetlocks and marched off, dragging Sam along behind her.

'I've got a list of people I don't like and you're going on it!' she called back over her shoulder to Apricot.

'We've all got lists, Giggles, so you can shove yours!' jeered Apricot, while Turbo and Mickey laughed like hyenas.

Mulberry did not say a word as they

made their way down to the bottom yard.
Sam let her back into her stable and as she
turned to go, Mulberry's scowling face
popped over the door.

'Bring me the show schedule two-legs and be quick about it!' she snapped.

Sam grinned and hugged herself with glee as she ran up to the office.

Chapter 9

Appealing to Mulberry's vanity was certainly the key to getting her to talk. Now Sam wished she could get her to shut up as all the mare did was complain.

'I am *not* doing the fancy dress competition,' Mulberry huffed. 'That's for the likes of those stupid Shetlands, dressed up like idiots, with their bellies dragging along the ground and horrible children sitting on their backs, picking their noses and eating their bogies. It's beneath my dignity.'

'*Everything* is beneath your dignity,' muttered Sam under her breath.

'What was that?' asked Mulberry, eyeing her suspiciously.

'Nothing,' said Sam. She looked at the show schedule again. 'How about Best Turned Out? You can't have any objections to entering that, surely?'

'Best Turned Out? Best Turned Out? Don't make me *laugh*!'

'What's wrong with Best Turned Out?'

'What's right with it? All you do is clean me, clean your tack, try not to spill anything on your show jacket, or get mud on your white jodhpurs and then we prance about around the arena with a bunch of other ponies and someone decides which of us is cleanest. I ask you—is that competing, *is it*?'

'Of course it is!'

'No, it's not, so stop being deliberately stupid. Best Turned Out is a competition that gets shoved into every show so the kids who can't ride to save their lives have a hope of going home with a rosette, and then their mummies and daddies can be proud of their useless children.'

'Mulberry!' gasped Sam, shocked at the mare's rudeness. 'That's a horrible thing to say!'

'Horrible but true,' she replied. 'The same kids picking their noses all the way through the Fancy Dress will be picking them again all the way through Best Turned Out. Just you wait and see. Although if you're planning on waiting and seeing *during* the competition you'd better get yourself a rocking horse, 'cause I won't be there.'

'Don't tell me—it's beneath your dignity.'

'Now you're catching on,' said Mulberry. 'And while we're on the subject of turnout, keep everything plain and simple, do *not* try putting ribbons on me.'

'Oh, but Mum bought some lovely green ribbons which would look beautiful in your black mane . . . ' said Sam.

'*No ribbons!*' Mulberry interrupted, snapping at the air with her teeth. 'Anything like a ribbon comes near me, I'm taking a lump out your bum the first chance I get.'

'Don't you think you're being just a little bit dramatic?'

'I am a native pony,' said Mulberry snobbily, sticking her nose in the air. 'Half Exmoor, half Welsh, one hundred per cent British. You show native ponies naturally. You don't trim my mane or tail, you leave it long and thick, and you can only use plain tack to show me in, no fancy bridles. We native ponies are naturally gorgeous and it is a crime against nature to mess with it . . . '

'OK, so no Fancy Dress, Best Turned Out, or ribbons. Is there anything else you object to?'

Mulberry thought for a moment. 'Dog's being off the lead, especially those yappy little ones.'

'No, Mulberry, about the show!'

'Is Best 50/50 Combination on the list?'

'Yes.'

'I'm not doing that either.'

Sam felt like flinging the clipboard on the ground and jumping up and down on it. 'Why not?!'

'Because it's another one of those pointless competitions,' said Mulberry. 'We walk and trot around the school, do a couple of circles, and a judge decides which of us is the best "partnership". Besides, it would be lying—I don't like you.'

Sam ran her eyes down the list again. 'Oh, this will be a good one, a basic dressage competition,' then her face fell. 'But because I'm under ten years old, we can't canter. But it would be good to give it a go. I love dressage!'

'Nope,' said Mulberry. 'It's just the Best 50/50 Combination competition again, but with a silly French name. Utterly pointless.'

'But that just leaves . . . ' Sam faltered as she read the show schedule.

'Yeeees?' wheedled Mulberry, her black eyes gleaming with delight.

'The Have A Go Jumping competitions,' said Sam, looking up at Mulberry. 'There are two of them and those jumps are big. The first competition is up to two feet and the second competition is up to two feet six inches.' Sam felt sick at the thought of trying to clear a jump that big.

'Now *that* is competing,' said Mulberry. 'You either get it right or get it wrong, you're either the fastest or the slowest, and you either win or lose. No messing about, none of this "every child wins a prize"

fluffy-wuffy thinking. There's just one problem.'

'What's that?'

'Show jumping is not your strong point. You are—how can I put this?—rubbish.'

'I am not!' said Sam indignantly.

'Oh yes you are!' said Mulberry. 'You fall forwards out of the saddle and onto my neck every time I land after a jump, because you don't sit back on the way down. Your balance is terrible and you grip the reins and keep pulling back when I try to go faster. Sock me in the mouth with the bit one more time and I'll lose a tooth! Honestly, I have an ache in my jaw every time you practise your jumping on me.'

'I'm just not very confident at jumping,' said Sam in a small voice. 'Can't we do the dressage competition?'

'No, we can't,' said Mulberry. 'This is what competing is all about. Riding well and riding fast to win. It's time to man-up, two-legs, and show the yard what you're made of. What we're made of, as a partnership.'

'But I'm scared I'll fall off,' said Sam.

'Pah!' said Mulberry curling her black lip in a sneer. 'It's not sport unless there is a chance of blood on the sand.'

'That's what I'm afraid of—I don't want it to be mine,' said Sam.

'What's the matter, don't you trust me?'

There is no polite way to answer that question, thought Sam.

Chapter 10

So Sam put her name down for the Have A Go Jumping competitions and *only* the Have A Go Jumping competitions. Amy gave her a funny look and Mum raised an eyebrow but did not say anything.

With just two weeks to go before the Meadow Vale Show, Mulberry insisted that they practise daily. So every day after school, Sam led Mulberry down to the outdoor arena and they practised circles, half halt, long loopy figures of eight, changing direction in canter, and of course jumping, until the dust from the arena coated Sam's hair and the inside of her throat, and dulled Mulberry's inky black coat.

Now that Mulberry had decided to co-operate, Sam did not have to worry about being dumped on the ground any more. There were no more nasty tricks and she could concentrate on her riding and getting to know Mulberry a bit better.

And they were getting better. The girls watching on the wall of the arena got quieter and quieter as they found themselves with less to say. Cecilia Jones and her friends had less ammunition for spiteful remarks. Sam began to relax on Mulberry's back, even when they whipped around corners so fast it took her breath away. Mulberry

never, ever slipped or hesitated. Every hoof beat was deliberate and perfect, even when she turned so fast she had to cross one leg over the other to keep her balance.

Whenever another person was around, Mulberry kept silent. But when it was just the two of them, she taught Sam just as well as Janey. 'Sit up,' she would say. 'Put your shoulders back and relax. Keep your hands quiet. And for pity's sake, you useless child, wrap your legs around me like you are giving me a hug and relax them! They are so stiff they are swinging backwards and forwards when they should be flat against my side. Look like a proper rider and don't make me look stupid!'

On top of Mulberry's advice Janey would shout, 'Keep your heels down and your toes up! Turn them in, you look like

Donald Duck when you stick your feet out. Lift your chin and look where you are going. Look for your turns—if you don't know where you are going how is Mulberry supposed to know? It's your job to tell her where to go. There's no point in turning for your jump at the last minute and pulling her head around at an angle to aim her for it. If you have to pull her head around that far, you are knocking her off balance!'

'And giving me a dreadful crick in my neck to boot,' grumbled Mulberry around her bit.

Jumping was still a problem. While her flatwork had improved in leaps and bounds, Mulberry still terrified her going over jumps. But Mulberry *loved* to jump. She bounded around like an over-excitable puppy when Janey or Amy set up jumps for Sam, shaking her head and practically frothing at the mouth. 'Oh goodie, oh goodie, *oh goodie!*' she would squeal as Sam tried to ignore the butterflies in her stomach.

As soon as Sam pressed her heels to Mulberry's side and gave her the command to canter, Mulberry took off at warp speed and leapt for the jump like a salmon out of water. She pushed herself off from the ground and curved in the air as she cleared a two-foot jump by at least another foot. She jumped so high her descent was very, very steep. Sam found it impossible to lean back fast enough to keep her balance and she fell against the mare's neck as soon as all four feet were on the ground. Mulberry was so excited she never waited for Sam to recover but charged straight into the next jump, with Sam struggling to get her balance back. That wonderful feeling of melting into each other, of being the same creature that twisted and turned and sped along as one, fell apart when they jumped.

The day before the show, Janey called a halt to her lesson after only ten minutes.

'There's no point doing too much with her today. You want her to be fresh as a daisy tomorrow and put on a good show,' said Janey. 'You are nearly there with the jumping. Just try and relax and go with her and you will get through tomorrow OK. You have to remember Sam, she knows her job. Let her get on with it and you'll both be fine. Don't stiffen up and hold onto her mouth, you'll only hold her back.'

Sam was exhausted from the days of

constant practise. Her neck, back, and shoulders ached from the riding and the grooming, and from polishing Mulberry's saddle and bridle until it shone. She felt like getting off Mulberry, handing the reins to Janey and telling Miss Mildew to stuff the Summer Show. She could quite happily spend tomorrow in bed, watching silly movies, and munching her way through a family-sized pack of crisps. Instead, she offered Janey a weak smile, 'I'll do my best,' she said.

'That you will,' said Janey. 'Fair do's Sam, you work hard and you're making a good job out of riding Mulberry. I didn't think you had it in you!'

'I'll do my best,' Mulberry mimicked Sam's voice on the way back to her stable. 'Lord help me, if that's the best you can do we're going to crash through every jump tomorrow.'

'Mulberry, give it a rest,' sighed Sam, as she took the saddle and bridle off the mare. 'You constantly having a go isn't doing much for my confidence. You could try to encourage me you know, that might work better than constant abuse.'

'Encourage you?' spat Mulberry. 'What have I been doing all this time? What do you call moving perfectly and not dumping you on your skinny bottom? What do you call ignoring the commands you give that are about as clear as mud and just doing what you meant to ask for anyway? I've been working my backside off in this heat. I've not put a foot wrong, and frankly, it's about time you started pulling your weight in this partnership!'

'I've been working hard, too!'

'Not really,' said Mulberry, narrowing her eyes at her. 'You might be willing to come down to the arena and go through the motions, but the truth is, two-legs, your mind is somewhere else. You mess up the jumping because you're thinking about all the things that can go wrong, all the possible ways you can get hurt, when I haven't done the slightest thing to make you doubt me.'

'That's not true!'

'Yes, it is. Think on this. Tomorrow could be my one chance to impress someone, to go to a good home and be ridden by a child who really wants to go out and win, and for me to have a home until the end of my days. So try thinking about that instead.'

'Oh, silly me,' said Sam. 'I forgot, I really should be thinking about you.'

'No, you should be thinking about us,' said Mulberry. 'It's meant to be a partnership.'

'So you keep saying,' said Sam. 'But I don't think you know what that really means.'

Mulberry flattened her ears and turned

her bum to Sam. 'It's you that doesn't know what it means,' she growled over her shoulder.

'Fine,' said Sam. 'Be like that!' She strode away with Mulberry's tack slung over her arm without a backwards glance.

Chapter 11

The sun beat down on the arena surface from a bright blue sky. Not a wisp of cloud drifted across its surface to give even a sliver of shade.

The show jumping competitions were the last on the show schedule, so Sam took her time getting Mulberry ready. She half listened to Janey's commentary, which sounded loud and clear over a tannoy, as the little ones paraded in the arena for the Fancy Dress and Best Turned Out competitions. She took her time brushing every speck of dust from Mulberry's velvety black coat and teased every knot and tangle from her thick mane and tail. She could hear the applause for the Dressage Competition as she oiled and polished Mulberry's hard little blue hoofs until they shone like wet slate. Mum had allowed Amy to ride Velvet for the dressage and Sam wondered how they were getting on as she carefully rubbed oil onto Mulberry's saddle and bridle, making the leather gleam. She should be there, supporting Amy, but she had told her sister she wanted to stay away from everyone until it was her turn to ride. Her nerves were a mess and she needed to be on her own, not out in the heat and the crowd. Amy had just shrugged and tweaked Sam's hair. 'You'll be fine, little monkey,' she had said. 'No need to hide.' But she was hiding and Amy was riding with only Mum for support. Sam felt bad but her hands were shaking. It was hard not to walk out there now and ask Mum to take her home.

Mulberry was still in a sulk after their argument yesterday and she did not say a word as Sam slipped the bridle over her head and the bit between her teeth. She snapped her teeth in irritation as Sam buckled up her girth.

When Mulberry was ready, Sam slipped away into the cool shade of the tack room on the bottom yard and changed into the clothes Mum had left for her there. She

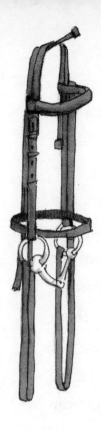

pulled on pale cream jodhpurs, a crisp white shirt, a neat black show jacket, and polished black boots. She smoothed her straight blond hair into a pony tail and knotted a tie around her neck. She carefully set her black velvet riding hat on her head and buckled a strap beneath her chin. She pulled snug riding gloves over her fingers and snapped the buttons closed around her wrists.

Picking up a short black riding whip, she strode out of the tack room and back to Mulberry's stable.

'Well, you certainly look the part,' said Mulberry as she looked Sam up and down. 'Very smart.'

'Thank you,' said Sam.

They were both solemn and quiet as they walked through the yard. Once they left the calm of Miss Mildew's personal stable block, chaos reigned. Riders ran in every direction as they tried to get ready for the show, their excitable mounts tied to the rails outside their stables, hopping from hoof to hoof. Grooming kits lay scattered all around, along with spare pieces of tack and the odd item of clothing. The yard looked as if a bomb had hit it.

Sam and Mulberry walked through it all, both lost in their own thoughts. Sam could see Apricot standing by the gate of the Shetlands' section of the barn but she was in no mood to talk to the little Shetland. She could see Basil shaking his head sadly as they passed. She squared her shoulders and went to join the rest of the riders lining up with their ponies by the side of the arena.

The show jumping course for the first competition was made up of seven jumps, with the biggest being two foot high. Sam was relieved to notice that some of them were quite small. What was going to make jumping the course difficult was the way it had to be ridden. Some jumps demanded that the pony and rider turn quite sharply before doubling back to make the next jump, while some demanded shallow turns if the partnership were to approach the jump dead centre. It could be dangerous to take the jumps at a tight angle or to jump too close to the sides. If the ponies could not see the jumps clearly as they cantered towards them, they were much more likely to refuse to jump at all or could jump badly, knocking poles down. It was a course that required more thinking than nerve.

Miss Mildew had given them the running order the day before and Sam would be the last to compete, while Amy would be the first. She lifted her eyes to the viewing stands. There were a lot of people sitting up there she did not recognize. A lot of people had travelled to the show so their children could compete and, of course, to look at any horses and ponies Miss Mildew had for sale. She wondered if any of them were looking at Mulberry right now? She could see Mum making herself comfortable on the hard wooden bench and she smiled and lifted her hand. Mum waved back and gave her a big thumbs up.

She looked up the line to see Amy standing with a pony called Neville, who loved to jump as much as Mulberry did. Amy cast an eye over Mulberry and mouthed 'She looks really good,' to Sam.

'Thanks,' Sam mouthed back and grinned at her sister.

Sam leaned into Mulberry and scratched her behind the ear. She tried to fight the feeling of panic that was already rising in her stomach as she whispered into her ear, 'We can do this, can't we?'

'Yes,' Mulberry whispered back. 'We can.' Then, to Sam's surprise, she pressed her shoulder against Sam's side and left it there, just for a moment. It was as comforting as a hug. Sam looked at Mulberry but the mare continued to stare straight ahead.

Janey announced Amy and Neville into the arena, the starter bell went and Amy rode Neville at break-neck speed into the first jump. Sam watched as Amy and Neville cleared jump after jump, Amy perfectly balanced on his back, Neville's hoofs tucked neatly beneath him as he leapt. They charged over the finishing line to deafening applause, not a single fence down.

Sam watched every rider, trying to learn the best way around the course from the way they rode. Cecilia Jones rode straight after Amy and cleared every jump too, galloping home just a little faster than Amy.

Some of the riders after that had rather more mixed fortunes. If the ponies knocked a pole down it counted as four faults. There wasn't a single pony and rider that managed to get a clear round after Amy and Cecilia. Poor Natalie managed to clock up twenty-four faults on Oscar, who seemed to enjoy making a fool out of her. Sam smiled nervously at Natalie as she made her shame-faced way out of the arena, tears filling her eyes.

Then it was her turn. She heard Janey announcing herself and Mulberry, and she swung up into the saddle, her legs trembling. She leaned down to pat Mulberry on the neck and heard her whisper, 'Don't worry, we've practised this loads of times.'

Mum always told her, 'Ride at home as

if you are competing and when you are competing, ride as if you were at home.' She basically meant the same thing as Mulberry—relax. But the arena stretched wider and wider as the sick feeling in her stomach got bigger and bigger, until it looked a hundred miles long. The sun beat down on her head and her gloved hands felt coated in sweat. Mulberry was excited as usual and pranced and jogged her way up to the starting line. Sam felt as boneless as a jellyfish as she bounced about on her back. She barely had time to get a better grip on the reins when the starter bell rang and Mulberry roared straight into canter from a standing start.

Sam forced her fear-stiff body into the jumping position as the first jump rushed towards them. Mulberry sprang lightly through the air but Sam panicked as she felt her balance wobble and she tipped back, catching the mare in the mouth as they landed. Mulberry shook her head in annoyance but powered on, taking the next jump as easily as Sam would step over a puddle.

This was the stage where they were supposed to double back on themselves and go over the third jump. Mulberry bent her body round and headed for it but Sam was slow to react and she wobbled in the saddle again. She didn't mean to do it, but as fear got the better of her, she pulled back on the reins, forcing Mulberry's head down just as she was taking off for the third jump. The little mare struggled to get her head up but she couldn't see where she was going and her front legs

clipped the top pole, bringing it crashing to the ground. Sam felt Mulberry falter as the crowd groaned, but the little black pony charged on.

Sam fought with her nerves and tried to relax in the saddle. She'd never felt so separate from Mulberry—the feeling of moving together was gone and she had to get it back, quick. It felt as if Mulberry was doing the course on her own and it was up to Sam to keep up. But she was so busy thinking about it she didn't get into the jumping position quick enough and was not prepared when Mulberry launched herself into the air. Again, she pulled on the reins and again Mulberry knocked a pole down, earning them both eight faults. She managed to regain her balance as the fifth jump loomed ahead but some of the energy seemed to go from Mulberry. Her jump over the sixth was half-hearted and another pole bounced to the ground, bringing their total to twelve faults. They cleared the last jump and cantered sedately across the finish line to polite applause. Sam was just relieved it was all over.

They had a half-an-hour break while the

jumps on the course were raised higher and the ponies were given a chance to get their breath back. Sam hurried Mulberry down to her stable, taking the long way round so they could avoid the Shetlands.

'My legs are killing me,' grumbled Mulberry as Sam led her down to the bottom yard. 'I'm going to be covered in bruises tomorrow, I whacked that many poles.'

'I thought it went OK,' said Sam. 'At least we got around.'

'It was dreadful,' said Mulberry. 'And it's all your fault.'

'How is it my fault?' asked Sam when they reached the cool of Mulberry's stable. She loosened the mare's girth to make her more comfortable and pulled her hat from her sweat-wet hair.

'Because you still don't trust me,' said Mulberry in a small, quiet voice.

'I do!'

'No, you don't,' said Mulberry. 'You still sit on my back and think "what if" all the time. *What if you fall, what if you hurt yourself,* instead of just trusting me to do my job and get on with it.'

'That's not strange Mulberry. It can be quite scary—' Sam began and then she stopped herself.

'Go on, say it!' demanded Mulberry. 'You were going to say it's scary riding *me*. I thought we had an understanding and I've taken good care of you the last few weeks and never dropped you, not once. And you have the cheek to tell me that *I'm* the one who doesn't know what partnership means.'

Mulberry's head drooped and her shoulders slumped. 'After that performance, who knows what kind of home I will end up in, if anyone wants me at all.'

'Oh Mulberry—' Sam felt a wave of guilt wash over her and she pulled her gloves off to stroke the mare's neck but Mulberry turned her back on her.

'Don't,' said Mulberry, her voice choked with sadness. 'Just leave me alone.'

Chapter 12

Sam did not know what to say to Mulberry as they made their way back down to the arena for the last competition of the day. Mulberry did not look at her. She hung her head and shuffled along, oblivious to the jeers of the Shetlands. All the fizz and pop had gone out of her as quickly as the air from a burst balloon.

I can't help being scared, thought Sam. *I try really, really hard, but it's just me. Why doesn't she understand?*

Mulberry stood quietly in the row, waiting for their turn to jump. She was so quiet Sam felt as if she were holding onto air, or had bridled up a wilted flower. The hated butterflies began to stir and flap their wings in her stomach and she tried to think positive thoughts as they took flight and whirled around her chest. She hardly noticed the other competitors as she tried to think about anything other than jumping. She scratched Mulberry behind the ear and stroked her face but the mare just looked at the ground and seemed to be in a world of her own.

What can I do? thought Sam frantically. *I can't be Amy, I can never be Amy.*

Another competitor left the arena to applause and a few cheers. The time for them to ride inched closer and closer. *Why do I do this?* Sam thought. *Why on earth do I keep doing something that scares me rigid a lot of the time?*

She looked up at the stands and saw Mum smiling at her. She thought of Mum and Velvet, not when they were riding but those moments before and after. Velvet dropping her head so Mum could brush her forelock and that spot behind her ears that always made Velvet close her eyes and nicker with pleasure when Mum rubbed it with a stiff brush. The way Velvet put her face against Mum's back and Mum would reach behind and stroke Velvet's cheek with the tips of her fingers, the two of them standing together so quietly. Or the way Velvet would prick up her ears and trot down to the gate when Mum called her, her face lit up with joy.

That's what I want, Sam realized. *I don't want to be Amy. I'm not even worried about being a great rider. I just want to find a pony I can love and who loves me.*

She looked at the dejected pony standing next to her and thought, *We're halfway there. I just need to take the next step.*

She jumped out of her skin as Janey announced that Sam and Mulberry were the next competitors to ride. As they walked up to the gate of the arena Sam

thought hard to find a way she could make things up to Mulberry in the next ten seconds.

She climbed into the saddle and while they waited for the starter bell to ring, she put a hand on Mulberry's neck and leaned down to whisper in her ear.

'You're right Mulberry, I didn't know what it meant to be in a partnership,' she said and she watched Mulberry's ears swivel back towards her. 'But I do now. And I do trust you, so I'm going to let you take care of both of us.' She tied a knot in her reins so they would not slip through her grip easily and held them with one hand. She wound the fingers of her other hand through the coarse hair of Mulberry's mane, and as she did so she felt the little mare stand up a little straighter.

Mulberry turned her head to look at her and whispered, 'What are you doing?'

'I'm going to close my eyes and just go with the flow,' said Sam.

'You're mad!' said Mulberry, her eyes sparkling with happiness.

'Just like you,' said Sam and she smiled at her.

The starter bell rang, Sam closed her eyes tight and kicked Mulberry into a canter. The mare took off and Sam felt her stomach turn over as they cleared the first jump. There were shouts of concern from the crowd when they realized she was riding with her eyes shut, but Sam blocked them out and thought only of the feel of Mulberry beneath her. With her eyes shut there were less distractions and she could feel every twitch of every muscle as Mulberry thundered around the course. Sam leaned away from Mulberry into every corner they ran through to balance her perfectly, and leant forward and back over every jump with perfect timing. As Mulberry twisted and turned through the course, gaining speed as her hard little hoofs threw up a cloud of dust, Sam felt that wonderful weightless feeling come back again, when every movement between the two of them was perfect and unplanned, and the safest place to be in the world was on Mulberry's back. As Mulberry bunched her muscles to leap over the last and biggest jump Sam felt as if they could rise into the sky like a song bird, climbing higher and higher into the clear blue.

She opened her eyes as Mulberry landed

sharply on the other side of the jump
and stood up in her stirrups as the mare
galloped for home. She pulled her to a
stop in the middle of the arena and the
whole yard exploded into applause. People
shouted, cheered, whistled, and stomped
their feet. Janey was jumping up and
down with joy while Miss Mildew just
stared at them, astonished. There was not
a single pole lying on the ground—they
had jumped a clear round.

'We did it!' said Sam.

Mulberry looked at her over her
shoulder. 'Told you,' she panted. 'Piece of
cake.' And she winked.

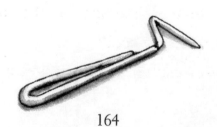

Chapter 13

O f course, they didn't win. That would
have been too much of a fairy-tale
ending and everyone knows they never
happen in real life. But second place to
big sister Amy was a pretty good result for
the day. Sam was smiling so hard as they
lined up for the prize giving in the arena,
she felt like her jaw muscles would snap
in two from the strain.

'What you just did was amazing,'
whispered Amy as they waited for Miss
Mildew to start handing out the rosettes.
'Stupid, but very cool!'

'It was, wasn't it?' Sam grinned and then

she thought for a second. 'Cool that is, not stupid.'

'Let's see what Mum thinks, shall we?' Amy giggled.

Miss Mildew stepped up with their rosettes. 'Congratulations, Samantha and Amy,' she said, not looking terribly pleased at all. She clipped Amy's first place rosette to Neville's bridle. 'Well ridden as usual, Amy.' She turned to Sam and clipped a red second place rosette to Mulberry's bridle, her lips tightening to a thin white line. 'I am delighted that all the expert tuition you have received here has paid off, Samantha,' she said in a clipped tone of voice. 'Well done.'

'Looks like I got my ribbons after all,' Sam whispered in Mulberry's ear as she dismounted. The little mare said nothing but she pulled a ferocious face and shook her mane. Sam giggled. Miss Mildew was taking her time pinning the third place rosette to the bridle of Cecilia's pony. 'So sorry to see you did not get your usual first or second place, Cecilia, but I am sure your talent and hard work will win out next time, as it should.' Cecilia was almost crying with rage and she glared at Sam with utter hatred. Sam quickly dropped her gaze to her hands.

Mum was waiting for them outside the arena as all the competitors walked out to applause and she grabbed Sam and crushed her in her chocolatey embrace.

'That was a very, very silly thing to do,' she said, as she hugged her tighter and kissed the top of her head. 'But it was very brave and wonderfully ridden. Well done.

I am so proud of you both.'

'And Mulberry,' said Sam. 'She did most of the work.'

'Yes, she did,' said Mum, digging around in her pockets for a treat. 'She looked magnificent out there today. I must say, the two of you know how to get the best out of each other.'

Mulberry sniffed at the piece of fluff-covered carrot Mum had unearthed from her pockets, before lipping it from her palm and chewing on it solemnly.

'I'm going to untack Mulberry, Mum, and cool her down. I'll be back soon,' said Sam.

'Yes, make her comfortable and we'll have our picnic,' said Mum. 'Don't dawdle now, either of you.'

Amy headed for the top yard to put

Neville back in his stable, while Mulberry and Sam walked to the barn. 'I know what you are thinking. Do we have to do this?' said Mulberry.

'I think Apricot deserves some thanks, don't you?' said Sam.

'Honestly? No,' said Mulberry. 'She's an interfering, stumpy-legged . . . '

'Shush!' said Sam, as Apricot, Mickey, and Turbo trotted excitedly to the gate.

'We saw, we saw everything from here, you were brilliant!' neighed Turbo.

'Well, it's as close as you're ever going to get to competing,' said Mulberry.

'Oh Mulberry, don't start!' said Sam. 'Apricot, I, well we, just wanted to say thanks for pairing us up. It's been a brilliant day.'

Apricot snorted. 'I didn't do it for you,

two-legs, or that flea-ridden bag of bones over there,' she huffed. 'I did it for revenge, pure and simple. Tell me,' she leaned close to the gate, her brown eyes gleaming with malice. 'How did Cecilia Jones take you beating her? Was she angry? Did she cry?'

Sam and Mulberry looked at each other. A simple humiliation was not going to be enough for Apricot and they both knew it. Mulberry's eyes sparkled as she looked at Sam, and Sam could just imagine Mulberry egging her on to tell a whopping lie. 'Yes, she was furious,' said Sam. 'She was actually crying with anger and she demanded to know who had fixed the competition in our favour and who had trained us. She couldn't believe we had beaten her. She said she had never been so humiliated in all her life.'

'I knew it!' neighed Apricot, rearing up on her back legs with excitement. 'That'll show her. Wait until the next show we've got coming up, oh, I've got plans for Miss Snobby Knickers—'

Basil wandered over to look at the Shetlands, who were skipping about their part of the barn with glee. He looked at

Sam and rolled his eyes. 'Mad, the lot of them.'

'Be quiet you and *get away from that fence,*' squealed Apricot as she charged, teeth snapping, at Basil's head.

Sam and Mulberry backed quietly away from the squabbling and walked off to the bottom yard, giggling as they went.

'He's right, you know,' said Mulberry. 'They're not right in the head. All Shetlands have a screw loose.'

Sam laughed. She led Mulberry into her stable, untacked her, and sponged the sweat from her coat. Then she topped up her manger with sweet-smelling hay and filled a bucket with fresh water. She leaned against Mulberry's shoulder and breathed in the smell of her in the cool peace of the stable as the mare munched away.

'I was just thinking,' said Mulberry through a mouth of hay. 'Do you reckon any one here today would be thinking of buying me?'

'I don't know,' said Sam, frowning. 'I think pretty much everyone knows Miss Mildew wants to sell you. You did great out there today, so maybe. Why, do you really want to go?'

Mulberry sighed. 'Well, I can't stay, can I? I'm not cut out to be a riding school pony. It's soooo boring, going around and around in circles until you feel dizzy, with some brainless child sitting on your back, kicking away because they don't know how to ride. It would be nice to go to a home and have just the one rider that I can train to do things my way and go out to competitions again. I miss competing.'

Sam twirled a lock of Mulberry's mane around her finger and felt tears sting the back of her eyes. She had managed to forget Mulberry was for sale over the last few weeks. It made her stomach ache to think that the fiery little mare could be gone in a week's time and Sam would never see her again.

Sam thought about the money she had in a bank account her parents had opened for her. All her birthday and Christmas money went into it and sometimes her grandparents gave her a little bit extra. The last time she had checked she had £150 saved up. *How much would it cost to buy Mulberry?* she wondered. Amy shared Velvet with Mum. Surely no one would mind if Sam had a pony of her own? Mum had said she would think about it if Sam found the right one.

But would Mum think Mulberry IS the right one? thought Sam. *She's pretty and fast and good at just about everything—but she's also grumpy and horrible!*

'Mulberry,' she said.

'Mmhpf,' snorted Mulberry as she ripped a piece of hay loose from her hay net. 'What?'

'What would you think if *I* bought you?'

Mulberry looked at her for a minute and then threw her head back and brayed like a donkey with laughter.

'What's so funny?' asked Sam, annoyed.

'It's a nice offer—for you!' said Mulberry. 'But honestly, it would take me *ages* to train you up. At my age, it's really not worth the hassle.'

'How old are you, exactly?'

'That, two-legs, is a very, very rude question to ask,' said Mulberry, as she swallowed her mouthful of hay. 'I thought you had more manners than that.'

Sam stared at her, open-mouthed—Mulberry, giving *anyone* a lesson in manners! The mare really did have a humungous ego.

'You really think you are something special, don't you?' said Sam, grinning.

'That's 'cause I am,' said Mulberry. 'Now run along and let me eat my dinner in peace.'

Sam laughed and checked her watch. 'I'm going but not because you said so. Mum has a picnic for lunch and I don't want Amy to eat all the chocolate before I get there. I'll see you tomorrow.'

She was walking away when Mulberry's

head popped over the stable door. 'Oi!'

'What?' said Sam.

'Any apples in this picnic of yours?'

Sam grinned. 'Possibly. Why do you want to know?'

'Because I reckon I deserve a treat after today, putting on a blinding performance and putting up with you and all that.'

'You think?' said Sam.

'Definitely,' said Mulberry. 'Only don't bring me any red ones, they're too sweet and make my teeth itch. Bring me a nice, tart green apple. And make sure it's crisp— no bad bits or bruises on it.'

'I'll see what I can do, your Majesty,' laughed Sam as she walked out of the bottom yard to find Amy and Mum.

'Nice kid,' said the horse in the stable next to Mulberry.

'Yeah, she's not bad,' said Mulberry. 'Not the brightest, but she's trainable.'

'Sounds like you're fond of her,' said the horse.

'Oh, I wouldn't go that far,' said Mulberry, burying her nose in her hay again.

MEET THE PONIES!

Mulberry

BREED: Exmoor X Welsh. Both Welsh and Exmoor ponies are native British breeds. Both breeds are renowned for being intelligent, which Mulberry definitely is—and she knows it, too! Welsh ponies are often very spirited and lively, like Mulberry, whereas Exmoor ponies tend to have kinder and gentler temperaments. Both breeds are very strong despite their small size, and are tough enough to live outside all year round.

HEIGHT: 12.2hh (a 'hand' is 4 inches. So Mulberry is 12 and a half hands high.)

COLOUR: Jet black   **MARKINGS:** None

FAVOURITE FOOD: Green apples (no bruised ones though—only the very best for this special pony!)

LIKES: Jumping, racing, and testing out riders to see how long they can stay on board!

DISLIKES: Ribbons of any kind, especially when people try and put them in her mane and tail. Also doesn't like silly little Shetland ponies who have got too big for their hoofs.

Velvet

BREED: Irish cob. Irish cobs are very sure-footed—making them really safe and comfortable to ride. They're exceptionally kind, very intelligent, and are big and strong, just like Velvet. Perfect for cuddles!

HEIGHT: 15.2hh

COLOUR: Black

MARKINGS: White star in between her eyes that looks like a big diamond.

FAVOURITE FOOD: Any treats, but especially carrots.

LIKES: Going for hacks in the countryside, and rolling in the field to have a good scratch all over!

DISLIKES: Flies

Apricot

BREED: Miniature Shetland pony. Shetland ponies originally come from the Shetland Islands in the very north of Scotland, although they're now found all over the world. Although they're the smallest native British breed, they're also the strongest (for their size). They are really brave, and tend to have very strong characters—which explains Apricot's feisty personality!

HEIGHT: 9hh

COLOUR: Dun with flaxen mane and tail. Dun is a warm shade of brown—like the colour of an apricot, and having a flaxen mane and tail is like having blonde hair.

MARKINGS: None

FAVOURITE FOOD: Hay, and lots of it!

LIKES: Being the boss!

DISLIKES: Silly humans—especially 'gibberers', and big horses who think they're important just because their heads are in the clouds.

POINTS OF A HORSE

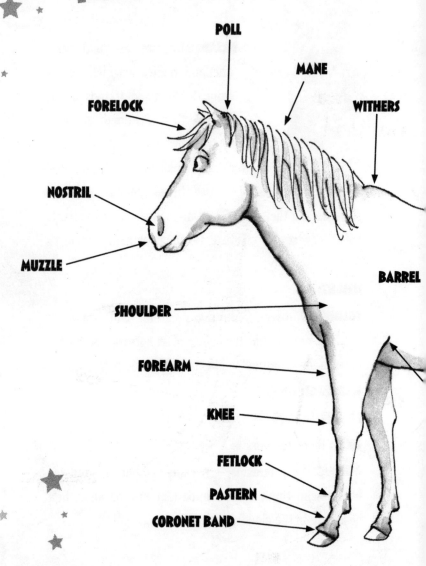

POLL

MANE

FORELOCK

WITHERS

NOSTRIL

MUZZLE

BARREL

SHOULDER

FOREARM

KNEE

FETLOCK

PASTERN

CORONET BAND

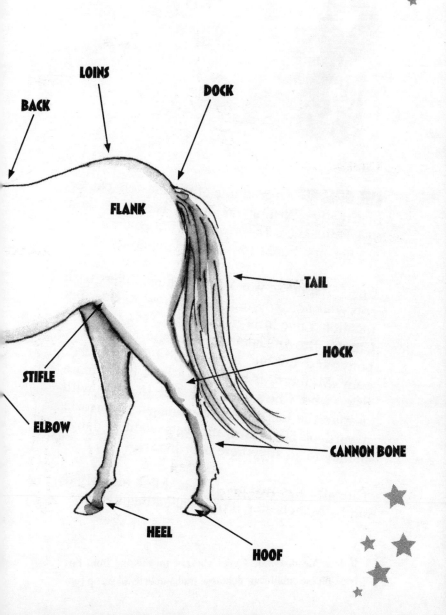

BACK

LOINS

DOCK

FLANK

TAIL

HOCK

STIFLE

ELBOW

CANNON BONE

HEEL

HOOF

© Lou Abercrombie from Abercrombie Photography

ABOUT THE AUTHOR!

CHE GOLDEN is a graduate of the Masters course in Creative Writing for Young People at Bath Spa University. *The Meadow Vale Ponies* series are her first books for Oxford University Press.

Che's first horse was Velvet, a huge, black Irish cob who not only taught Che how to ride, but taught her two little girls as well. Now, they own Charlie Brown, a rather neurotic New Forest pony, and Robbie, a very laid-back Highland pony. Mulberry is based on a little black mare, Brie, who Che's daughter fell in love with, despite the fact that Brie managed to terrorize a yard of 50 horses and vets wanted danger money to go anywhere near her.

Che also has two pet ferrets, Mike and Mindy, and a Manchester Terrier called Beau Nash.

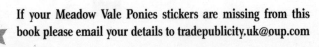

If your Meadow Vale Ponies stickers are missing from this book please email your details to tradepublicity.uk@oup.com